PUFFIN BOOKS

THE GHOSTS OF COBWEB

Catherine Sefton is the pen-name of Martin Waddell. He has written many books for children of all ages. He has won a number of awards including the Smarties Prize, The Kurt Maschler Award, The Other Award and was a runner-up for the *Guardian* Children's Fiction Prize. He now lives by the sea in Northern Ireland with his wife, three sons and their dog, Bessie.

CATHERINE SEFTON

The Ghosts
of Cobweb

Illustrated by Jean Baylis

PUFFIN BOOKS

PUFFIN BOOKS

Published by the Penguin Group
Penguin Books Ltd, 27 Wrights Lane, London W8 5TZ, England
Penguin Books USA Inc., 375 Hudson Street, New York, New York 10014, USA
Penguin Books Australia Ltd, Ringwood, Victoria, Australia
Penguin Books Canada Ltd, 10 Alcorn Avenue, Toronto, Ontario, Canada M4V 3B2
Penguin Books (NZ) Ltd, 182–190 Wairau Road, Auckland 10, New Zealand

Penguin Books Ltd, Registered Offices: Harmondsworth, Middlesex, England

The Ghosts of Cobweb first published by Hamish Hamilton Ltd 1992
The Ghosts of Cobweb and the Skully Bones Mystery first published by
Hamish Hamilton Ltd 1993
Published together in Puffin Books 1994
1 3 5 7 9 10 8 6 4 2

Printed in England by Clays Ltd, St Ives plc
Filmset in Baskerville

Chapter One

Sir Richard's ghost was in the kitchen, where we expected to find him.

"We need to speak to you, Sir Richard," my mum said.

"In the interests of the younger ghosts of Cobweb village!" I said, hurriedly, in case he might disappear.

"Cobweb is no place to bring up a decent young ghost," snorted Sir Richard. "Nothing is where it used to be."

"Not even the floor!" said my mum.

She shouldn't have said it. Sir Richard's ghost is easily annoyed, and just then he was floating six inches above where our real nowadays floor is, at the point where the floor used-to-be, in his day.

He snorted, and floated down to our floor level.

"Why did you move it?" he barked.

"We didn't," my mum said, patiently.

"The floor was lowered about two hundred years after you d . . . about a hundred years ago," I said. "I've told you that trillions of times. Don't you remember?"

Just then the washing machine took one of its turns.

It isn't much of a washing machine. It roars and grunts and shakes when it has a mind to, just like Sir Richard. Sir Richard ought to be used to washing machines by now, like the other ghosts in Cobweb, but he isn't.

WRRRRRRRRRRR-RUUUSSSH! went the washing machine, and Sir Richard shot up in the air, hitting his head on the ceiling. That brought him down again, sharpish. It was the original Sir-Richard's-time ceiling, so he knew all about it being there. At least, if he didn't, he soon found out when his ghostly head hit it.

4

"Are you all right, Sir Richard?" Mum asked anxiously.

Sir Richard had gone pale, and flickerish, and we absolutely didn't want him to disappear before we'd got talking to him.

It is a bad sign when a ghost gets the flickers, especially one of the older ghosts, like Sir Richard.

He opened his mouth, and seemed to be complaining about his sore head, but nothing came out when he spoke. That sometimes happens to our ghosts. They seem to go off channel, like TV sets. You get the picture, but not the sound.

He started to float up the stairs . . . *his* stairs, I mean. There aren't any stairs in our kitchen now, but there used to be in his time, and so he still floats up them.

"Stop!" Mum shouted. "Sir Richard, we've got to talk to you. It is really most important . . ."

But Sir Richard had gone.

"Great!" Mum said, sitting down in her chair. "Now what do we do, Jackie?"

6

"Don't know!" I said, because I
didn't.

We needed to talk to Sir Richard
about our school, Cobweb Primary,
where my mum teaches.

Cobweb isn't much of a place,
because there aren't many people in
in it, not more than two hundred, not
counting the ghosts. That isn't fair,
because we do count the ghosts (or
we would count them, if we could
spot them all at once, but they are on
and off ghosts. We don't get them all
about at one time). Anyway, it
doesn't matter whether we count the
ghosts, because the Education Board
doesn't, and the Board pays for the
school.

The School Inspector was coming

to close our school.

My mum reckoned that was what
he was going to do. He said he was
coming to inspect it, but she said
that that meant close it. If he closed
it that would mean we'd have no
school and all of us would have to go
somewhere else, on a special bus.
That was bad, but what was worse
was the ghosts. If he closed the

school in Cobweb, our young ghosts
would get no education.

You couldn't persuade our ghosts
to go on a special bus, and even if
you could there wouldn't be room for
them. Ghosts need their own ghost-
spaces to be in, just like people, and
there wouldn't be enough ghost-
spaces on the bus.

"We've got to show them our
school is too good to close!" my mum
said, when she first heard about it,
and I said, "What about *them*?"

I meant our ghosts, the ghosts of
Cobweb.

We've got good ghosts, as ghosts
come and go. As far as our ghosts are
concerned they are still people,
like anybody else. It is just that the

world around them has gone a bit
wonky, and peculiar.

"If the School Inspector hears
about our ghosts he'll close Cobweb
School down for sure!" my mum
said.

"Why?" I said.

"Because he'll say everybody in
Cobweb is mad for believing in
ghosts," Mum said. "He won't want
a batty school, with a batty teacher!"

"He'd better not hear about them,
then," I said.

That was why we had to speak to
Sir Richard, but it didn't work, Sir
Richard being Sir Richard.

"We'll just have to try explaining
to the others," I said. "They'll have
to lie-low till the School Inspector

has been and gone."

"You try telling them that,
Jackie!" my mum said.

So I did.

Chapter Two

"Now you listen to me!" I said. "I didn't come all the way out here for nothing. This is very important."

I was out at the crossroads . . . *their* crossroads, that is. It isn't a crossroads now, because the little road that crossed the main road to Hamly vanished years ago, somewhere in the middle of Ben Yardle's fields. Even the main road isn't the main road any more. It is not much more than a lane really.

You get to Hamly quicker by using the by-pass.

So far as our ghosts are concerned, all of that never happened. They hang about where their crossroads used to be.

"This man's coming," I said. "He's from the Education Board. He's coming to look at the school. We want everything nice, everything fine, so that we can really impress him. If he doesn't like Cobweb School, he'll close it!"

That set the ghost of the Old Minister flickering like mad. Stan Yardle, who was our Ben Yardle's Great-Great-Grandad, had to thump him to get his breath back. The Old Minister took it hard, because he

opened our school, the first day, back
in 1853.

Some of the young ghosts,
Nicholas and Ruth and Hannah Lee,
started giggling and laughing and
mucking about, saying they didn't
mind if there was no school, but the
Old Minister soon shut them up.

"So we want you all to be good
ghosts, while the man is here, and not
go getting up to anything," I said.

14

Some of them were offended, being
respectable ghost-people. They
didn't see why any man from the
City should come teaching them to
behave. Old Lottie Barwistle was
going to argue, I saw that coming,
and so was Henry Wilks who is a
very good-living-reading-his-Bible-

ghost; but it wasn't the well-behaved ones I was worried about.

"You tell that to Tom Baty," I said. "Young Tom and *old* Tom, in particular. None of their tricks."

That set a lot of ghost-heads nodding.

Henry Barwistle, old Lottie's nephew, started in about the time young Tom Baty stole the cheese off Stan Yardle's auntie and Stan Yardle said his auntie had never been the same since and the Old Minister started shaking his head and pacing up and down and young Nicholas said he would see to young Tom Baty, which didn't impress anybody. Tom Baty *is* Tom Baty, and all the ghosts knew he would make three of

Nicholas, who is pale and spindly, even for a ghost. Anyway, it wasn't just young Tom. There was old Tom as well.

If young Tom is tricky, old Tom is trickier.

They are the trickiest pair of ghosts I know, and bad-tempered as well, almost as bad-tempered as Sir Richard.

I left the ghosts all putting their heads together at the crossroads, and went back to our house.

"Did you tell them, Jackie?" Mum said.

"Yes, Mum," I said.

"What about the two Toms?" she said.

"They weren't about, Mum," I said. "I suppose they were off making trouble somewhere else."

That was the real cause of the bother. I never did get talking to the two Toms, and by the time the School Inspector showed up, it was too late.

Chapter Three

"Mrs Ogle?" the School Inspector said.

"That's me," my mum said. "You're Mr Quick?"

"Very pleased to meet you, I'm sure," the School Inspector said, and he shook my mum's hand with one of those weak, wristy handshakes that mean nothing at all.

He'd come from the City in his nice new car, and parked it out in front of Cobweb Primary School, on the Long Grass.

That was a mistake for a start.
Anyone who knew Cobweb could
have told him that.

The Long Grass used to be Batys'
land, before the Old Minister built
the school. The Old Minister bought
it off the last of the Batys, William
Thomas Baty in 1851, and the rest of
the Batys, that is the ones who were
already ghosts, the two Toms,
weren't one bit pleased. The two
Toms made trouble for eighty years
or so after the school was built and
then they gave up trying, and started
haunting the Church Hall and the
Dog and Whistle instead. There were
a lot of tough kids at Cobweb School
around 1930 and my Grandad Ogle

reckons he and his friends were too tough for the two ghostly Toms.

Still, the Long Grass is Batys' Long Grass, as far as the Toms are concerned. When my mum saw where the School Inspector had parked his car, she tried to suggest he should move it, but he wouldn't listen.

"Quick by name and quick by nature, Mrs Ogle," he said. "I'll just nip in and take a look at the facilities, and then I'll be on my way to the Scrobe School."

The Scrobe School is ten miles away, in High Easton. We thought that that was where most of us would be sent in buses, if he closed our school down. *Us*, that is, not the ghosts. Even if there hadn't been the problem about ghost-spaces on the buses, I can't imagine any of the Cobweb ghosts putting up with being sent to school in foreign parts. High Easton is only ten miles away, but it might as well be the other side of the world as far as our ghosts are concerned. Our ghosts are *Cobweb* ghosts, they belong in their own place, and they don't hold with foreign travel.

The School Inspector came into the school.

We all sat there, all fifteen of us, *real* children, not the ghost sort. We'd persuaded the ghosts to keep out of the way, and my mum had given them special writing to do, on their slates, to keep them busy. If you listened carefully you could hear the scrape of the chalk on their slates in the cloakroom, where they were hidden, out of the way. It is a funny noise, that. It gets on my nerves. We tried to teach them writing with ballpens and exercise books like everybody else, but they didn't take to it. Even our young ghosts are set in their ways . . . something to do with being ghosts, and a bit old-fashioned, I suppose. It was chalk and slates in their day, and that is the way they expect it to be.

"Very cramped for space, Mrs Ogle!" the School Inspector said, and he wrote something down in his notebook.

"We manage very well," my mum said.

"Um," said the School Inspector.

Then he looked at our lavatories, and went "Um" again, and wrote something down, and scored under it very heavily.

"The local children are very fond of this school," Mum said, beginning to get desperate. There are ways of saying "um" that give·it different meanings, and the School Inspector's "um" was the sort of "um" that means what-a-useless-old-school-this-is.

"The Scrobe School has been enlarged recently," the School Inspector said. "I'm sure your children would appreciate a nice new building."

"Not if it means ten miles either way in the bus," my mum said, stoutly. "Anyway, these are Cobweb children, Mr Quick. They deserve a school in their own village, and they've got one!"

"I'm sure the transport provided
will be excellent!" the School
Inspector said.

That's when I said, "We're not
going to the Scrobe School!"

Just like that.

Everybody cheered!

My mum looked cross, only not
really cross. There are ways of
looking cross that mean "you-
tell-'em, Jackie," and the School
Inspector knew it.

"Um!" he said, and he looked daggers at my mum, and she looked daggers back at him.

Then he marched out of the school to drive off in his car to inspect the brand new buildings at the Scrobe School in High Easton, and tell the teachers there that our school in Cobweb was no use.

That is what he meant to do, but he didn't get doing it.

His new car was in the duckpond.

Chapter Four

"This is an outrage!" the School Inspector said. He was really mad at his car being moved.

He went pink and white, both at the same time, and his little eyes gleamed behind his glasses, and he bounced over to the duckpond.

I should explain about the duckpond.

The thing is, he didn't know it *was* a duckpond.

It doesn't look like a duckpond,

because there are no ducks there any more, except a few ghostly ones who appear sometimes on a Sunday, when it is hot. There's no water either, just long weeds and mud that doesn't look like mud until you are in it.

He found out, when he fell in it.

He didn't so much fall as slither, and sit down.

And sink.

He didn't sink very far, but it was far enough.

He came up, grasping the back wheel of his new car, and gasping.

We all started cheering, and then we stopped because it wasn't funny, really. We could all see my mum's face. She had her our-last-hope-has-gone-now face on.

"You'll hear more about this, Mrs Ogle!" The School Inspector said, and he climbed into his car, making the driver's seat all muddy, and tried to start the engine.

I didn't know that the two Toms knew *anything* about motor-car engines, which were a long way after their time, but they are clever ghosts, even if they are bad, tricky ones. They must have picked up a few tips when they were poaching over the motorway (which is where Sir Richard's pheasants used to be kept).

Anyway, the Toms had fixed the car.

Actually, they'd *un*fixed it.

The car wouldn't start.

It wouldn't budge when he tried to push it, either.

"Somebody might at least try to help me!" he shouted.

And *somebody* did.

Chapter Five

It takes a lot of muscle to move a car
that is stuck in the mud of a used-to-
be duck pond. Not the sort of muscle
that you find on my mum, or a load
of kids.

You need a cart horse.

But we hadn't got a cart horse.

All we'd got was Sir Richard's
charger, that he rode on in his last
battle. It wasn't a good battle, from
Sir Richard's point of view. His
side lost, and we think Sir Richard

got killed. Anyway he didn't show up back at Cobweb until nearly a hundred years later, and then he came plodding over the fields on his horse, all blood and tatters, and half scared the rest of our ghosts to death.

Sir Richard's horse has been around a long time, but the Old Minister went and got it, and we hitched it up, and it pulled and pulled . . . I don't know what the trouble was, but perhaps, being a ghost horse, it didn't have the pull it used to have.

Still, with Sir Richard's horse, and the Old Minister, and Stan Yardle and Henry Barwistle and the two Toms . . . my mum collared them and *made* them help . . . we shifted the car.

Our ghosts moved the car, but
they couldn't move the man.

He just sat in the car and stared at
them. Then he took off his glasses
and stared, and then he put his
glasses back on, and stared again.

Then he said, "I don't believe
this!"

"What's that, Mr Quick?" my mum said.

"I can see through them!" he said. "They're g-h-o-s-t-s!"

He'd gone all pale and shivery.

"I don't know about being ghosts," old Lottie Barwistle said, floating round the side of his car. "But ghosts or no ghosts you might still say thank you!"

Lottie is a stickler for politeness.

I don't suppose Mr Quick had ever been spoken to by a ghost before.

He took it badly.

He screamed, and leapt out of his car and ran away.

We don't know what happened to him, but he never put in his report saying that our school ought to be closed, and he never came back for his car.

His nice new car is in the Long Grass still, on the far side of the duckpond, where our ghosts left it after they had pulled it out for him.

Sometimes, when we are on our way home from Cobweb School on a winter's evening, we see the two

Toms sitting in it, with young Hannah Lee in the back seat. They don't know how to drive it yet, but we reckon they are both interested.

That would be just like the two Toms.

Anyway, my mum has given them a copy of the Highway Code, and the kids at Cobweb School are making them a brand new set of "L" plates for Christmas."

The Ghosts of Cobweb
and the
Skully Bones Mystery

For Jamie

1. *Skully Bones*

"Skully Bones?" said Sir Richard, flickering a bit, the way our ghosts do when they are worried or upset.

"Skully Bones!" my mum said angrily. "Who is "Skully Bones" and what is he doing messing up my kitchen?"

Sir Richard reached for his sword.

I grabbed our budgie, Helmut, from his cage, just in case Sir Richard started waving his sword about. Having a ghost sword pass through you can be a bit upsetting, even for a sensible budgie who knows all about ghosts.

Everybody in Cobweb is used to ghosts. We have to be, because there are so many of them about. There must be something odd about Cobweb that makes it not-like-other-places where people don't see ghosts every day of the week.

We do.

There are lots of ghosts in Cobweb: Nicholas and Ruth and Hannah Lee and other young ghosts who go to our school, and their relations and ancestors wandering about the place. Most of them are good, respectable, pass-the-time-of-day ghosts. The two we worry about are the Tom Batys, Young Tom and Old Tom, who play tricks and mess about. Lottie Barwistle says they were just like that when they were alive, so nothing much has changed.

"No swishing, Sir Richard!" my mum said.

Sir Richard stopped swishing his sword, and looked hurt.

"I was only trying to help," he said, sounding confused.

"Swishing your sword about doesn't help anybody!" Mum said firmly.

"Skully Bones. . . ?" Sir Richard said, still fingering his sword in its scabbard. "If Skully Bones is here . . . ."

"Mum doesn't mean *is* here," I said hurriedly. "She means Skully Bones *was* here."

"Who is Skully Bones?" said Sir Richard, looking puzzled.

"That's what we are asking you, Sir Richard," Mum said patiently. "Jackie and I want to know who has been messing up our kitchen!"

She showed him the writing on our fridge.

It said:

Then we told him about all the other "Skully Bones" messages that somebody had written up round the village. Things like "SKULLY BONES RULES OK" and "SKULLY BONES 16 – WORLD XI 0" and "SKULLY BONES IS WORLD CHAMPION". Skully Bones signs were all over Cobweb, and we didn't like them.

"We won't have it, Sir Richard!" my mum said fiercely.

"This Skully Bones joke isn't funny, Sir Richard," I said, backing her up, and Helmut gave a budgie chirp to show he didn't like it either.

Sir Richard flickered anxiously, and looked as if he was going to disappear, which is what our ghosts do when things begin to get awkward.

"No disappearing, Sir Richard!" my mum said. "I've tried my best for the ghosts in this village, but they have got to behave themselves just like everybody else. If ghosts are going to go around writing silly messages on walls something will have to be done."

Then she banged out of the kitchen, slamming the door because she was so angry.

The door slam startled Helmut the budgie, but it was much worse for Sir Richard. Our ghosts get moved about by air currents when a door slams, and Sir Richard floated up near the ceiling.

Then he floated down to just above floor level, quivering. Mum frightens Sir Richard sometimes when she is cross, although she is a nice, gentle mum really.

"You have to do something, Sir Richard," I said. "Or there will be rows and rows and rows."

He flickered and disappeared, which wasn't very helpful, although it was typical Sir Richard.

That is when I decided I would have to solve the Mystery of Skully Bones all by myself.

2. *Council of War!*

"Disgraceful!" the Old Minister said.

"I don't know what the world is coming to!" Lottie Barwistle muttered.

"Young ghosts aren't what they used to be!" said old Henry Wilks, and he frowned at Hannah Lee and young Nicholas who were trying to look like very-sensible-young-ghosts, which they aren't.

'Hmmph!' said Henry Barwistle, old Lottie's nephew.

I'd gone down to *The Dog and Whistle* to catch all our ghosts together. *The Dog and Whistle* isn't a pub any more. It is just a ruin down Yardle's Lane but they still haunt it out of habit, even though the very young ones aren't allowed to go inside. The old ones like it, although the two Tom Batys complain about the beer, which isn't as good as it used to be.

"It is up to you to stop Skully Bones!" I said. "Cobweb is a nice village. We don't want ghosts going round writing silly things on walls and spoiling everything."

Stan Yardle shimmered a bit, and looked annoyed.

"Might be *people* doing it!" he said. "Not ghosts at all!" Stan is touchy about ghosts-being-blamed-for-things. It happens a lot in Cobweb.

People looking for an excuse say
something like, "Must be the ghosts
again!" and it makes our ghosts
really mad, especially Stan.

"Skully Bones?" I said. "That's
ghosts!"

"We haven't got skulls and
bones," Lottie pointed out. "Not
exactly. We're more like *shapes*
nowadays, with not-a-lot inside. Not-
a-lot that is *solid*, anyway."

"You speak for yourself, Lottie
Barwistle!" Stan Yardle said.

I didn't want to get mixed up in
another of their arguments, because
it wasn't going to help me solve the
Mystery of Skully Bones. I thought I
knew who was doing it anyway, so I
said so.

"It *could* be people," I admitted. "On the other hand, it is much more likely to be You-Know-Who!"

That stopped them.

"Young Tom . . ." frowned the Old Minister.

". . . or Old Tom," said Lottie.

"Or both Toms!" said Henry Barwistle.

"Right!" I said. "If it is the Tom Batys messing about, it is up to you to find them and stop them."

"Why?" demanded Stan Yardle. "Why is it up to us?"

"Because you are the Ghosts of Cobweb!" I said. "You are decent, friendly, respectable, good-living ghosts with a reputation to live up to, and Cobweb is *your village!*"

"Quite right!" said Henry Wilks.

"Put that in your pipe and smoke it, Stan Yardle!" Lottie Barwistle cackled.

"Hunt the Batys!" shouted Hannah Lee and Nicholas, jumping up and down with excitement.

And that is how the Great Baty Hunt began.

3. *The Great Baty Hunt*

Ghosts dashing about are like a lot of
little breezes.

Lots of little breezes everywhere.

That is what the Great Baty Hunt
was like.

Normally, that kind of thing
happens at night. There is a very
good reason for that, but you have to
think to understand it. It is to do
with ghost-space. Most people don't
like being walked through by ghosts
. . . it is a chilly feeling . . . but

ghosts don't much like being walked through by people either.

When the Great Baty Hunt began it was daytime and a lot of ghosts dashed through a lot of people.

It led to upsets.

Sir Richard rode right through Mr Stephens when he was driving his tractor, and the sudden chilly rush made him drive into the ditch.

Nobody knows what it did to Sir
Richard, but we didn't see him about
the place for the next half hour, while
he was recovering from the shock.

I think it was Lottie Barwistle who
dashed through the cow. I don't
know, because the cow didn't say,
but whoever was dashing gave a
Lottie-like squeak, so I think it was
her.

I know it was the Old Minister
who dashed through my mum and
made her upset her shopping trolley,
because he appeared very quickly
and apologised and helped her pick
things up.

It was very funny to watch, even if we didn't know which ghost was doing the dashing.

One ghost ran through Ben Yardle's field, breezing a path through the corn, and then another ghost chased after it. I think the other ghost, the chasing one, was Stan Yardle. Stan still thinks Ben Yardle's field is his, and he wasn't going to have anybody trespassing. They chased each other round in circles for ages.

Another ghost must have fallen in
the river. I knew about that because
I followed the drips down the street
on the way back from the bridge, and
I could hear the ghost-sneezes.

Ruth and I watched and waited. Ruth isn't like the other young ghosts. She is quieter than Hannah Lee and Nicholas, who can be really silly ghosts sometimes, when they think they can get away with it. They pretend to be goody-goody ghosts and go round as if butter wouldn't melt in their mouths, but they are almost as tricky as the Batys.

I knew if anyone was going to help me solve the Skully Bones Mystery it would be Ruth.

We decided we would be Skully Bones Detectives, and we waited and watched the way good detectives do.

4. *Ghost Detectives*

Ruth and I were standing in front of the Church Hall watching the drips go down the lane after whichever-ghost-fell-in-the-river when I turned round and saw:

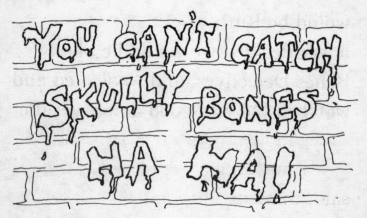

on the Hall wall.

"Look at that!" I gasped. "Skully Bones strikes again!"

"*That* wasn't *there* a minute ago!" Ruth said.

"How do you know?" I asked.

"Because I remember it wasn't," Ruth said, looking very serious. "Somebody sneaked up behind us when we weren't looking and did it. So it *must* have been a ghost, mustn't it?"

"Why must it?" I said.

"Because real people are so noisy!" she said.

I *thought* a bit. It had to be someone tall to reach as high as that, and stupid enough to want to do it.

"It must have been a tall ghost," I said, thinking out loud.

"Or a ghost up a ladder," Ruth said. "Only there isn't a ladder."

"How about a *ghost*-ladder?" I said. "It would be typical of the Toms to have a ghost-ladder hidden away somewhere."

That was when Sir Richard and the Old Minister arrived, covered in mud, dragging along behind them two mud-stained Tom Batys, tied up in the Old Minister's bell rope.

"Caught them!" Sir Richard cried. "Skully Bones is unmasked!"

"It wasn't us!" the two Toms cried. They were cross, and dripping mud at every step.

"Don't lie to me, you devils!" cried Sir Richard, feeling for his sword. "I didn't chase you right through Dogweed Marsh for nothing!"

"Not us! Not us!" the two Toms shouted.

"Yes it was! Yes it was!" yelled Sir Richard.

"No, it wasn't," Ruth said.

"What do you mean, child?" said the Old Minister, gently. He knows Ruth is sensible, and he always listens to her.

"While you were chasing the Tom Batys, *someone* wrote "YOU CAN'T CATCH SKULLY BONES HA HA!" up on the wall behind us!" Ruth said, and she showed the Old Minister what we'd seen.

"Not us! Not us!" the two Toms cried, bounding about. They are so used to being blamed for everything that I suppose being not guilty of something was a whole new experience.

All the ghosts had gathered round by now.

I looked at them.

Then I knew who Skully Bones was!

5. *Skully Bones Unmasked!*

"I know who Skully Bones is!" I
shouted.

Everybody gasped.

"I've just remembered!" I said.
"We heard about him ages ago, *didn't
we, Ruth*?

Then I winked at Ruth, hard.

"Oh . . . er, yes," Ruth said,
looking worried, because she had no
idea what I was talking about, but
she knows a wink when she sees one.

"Hannah Lee and Nicholas know

about him too, don't you?" I said, looking hard at them.

Hannah Lee gulped.

"Y-e-s," said Nicholas, flickering a bit.

"Who is it?" demanded the Old Minister.

"It is SKULLY BONES!" I said.

"We know it is Skully Bones!" Lottie Barwistle said. "Stop playing games, Jackie. What we don't know is *who* Skully Bones *really* is."

"Skully Bones *is* Skully Bones," I said. "Skully Bones the very-big-very-bad-highwayman who was hanged at Potts' Cross."

"Who?" said Lottie.

"Never heard of him!" said the Old Minister.

"We have," said Hannah Lee,
quickly. "We heard all about him in
. . . in . . ."

"In school," I finished off for her.
"My mum taught us all about him
when we were doing our Local
History Project, didn't she,
Nicholas?"

"Yes," said Nicholas, going red, which is difficult for a ghost, because they are a bit pale usually. "Yes, she did."

The other ghosts looked doubtful.

"Skully Bones was probably before your time," I said to them and that pleased them, because they all like to think they are younger than they really are. Any ghost would, I suppose.

"It will be all right," I went on,
"because Hannah Lee and Nicholas
and Ruth and I saw somebody who
looked just *exactly* like Skully Bones
and we chased him. He won't be
coming back, so there won't be any
more Skully Bones messages! Will
there?"

I stopped. Then, I looked hard at
Hannah Lee and Nicholas. "There
won't be any more messages, will
there?" I repeated.

80

Hannah Lee and Nicholas gulped, and nodded their heads.

I don't know if the grown-up ghosts believed me. They wandered off grumbling about it, all except the two Tom Batys, who were so pleased at *not* being to blame for something that they didn't grumble at all.

"What was all that about, Jackie?" Ruth said, when we were alone with Nicholas and Hannah Lee.

"A Great Big Silly Ghost called Skully Bones," I said. "Big enough to reach high up walls. The kind of ghost who might almost be *two* small ghosts, one standing on the other's shoulders."

"But . . . but . . ." Ruth stammered.

"But I'm sure no ghosts round here would play stupid tricks like that," I said, winking at Nicholas and Hannah Lee. "And if they did, one of them would absolutely *not* stand in the paint and leave footprints on the other one's shoulders."

This time, Ruth understood!

"I'm sure if *any* ghosts round here
played a silly joke like writing
"Skully Bones" on walls they would
be very sorry for doing it. They

would clean all the Skully Bones writing off the walls straight away, even if it took them ages to do it," she said.

"And make it up to the Batys for being chased!" I added.

That is why all the "Skully Bones" messages in Cobweb were cleaned up so neatly, and why the Batys got fresh ghost-eggs (from Hannah Lee's ghost-hens) and lots of ghost-wood chopped and left outside their ghost house, by a ghost-they-never-saw. The two Toms were very pleased.

It is also why Skully Bones was never heard of in Cobweb again.

THE GHOST

FAMILY ROBINSON

Martin Waddell

"You know the Robinsons don't like being lonely," I said. "They'd be frightened in your house, all on their own."

The Robinsons are not ghosts who like being left alone. And they don't like not being believed in either, as Tom's parents find out when the Robinsons come to stay.

Also in Young Puffin

CLASS THREE AND THE BEANSTALK

Martin Waddell

A GIANT beanstalk and a BIG surprise!

Class Three's project on growing things gets out of hand after they plant a packet of Jackson's Giant Bean seeds. The resulting beanstalk keeps growing...and growing...and growing...
Wilbur Small is coming home! Everyone is delighted and making great preparations. All except for the Grice family who are new and don't know what all the fuss is about...

Also in Young Puffin

Ricky's Summertime Christmas Present

Frank Rodgers

**FOR RICKY BROWN. DO NOT WAIT
UNTIL CHRISTMAS. OPEN NOW!**

Ricky is puzzled to receive a Christmas
present in the middle of summer from an
uncle he didn't know he had. But the
present leads him on an exciting
adventure to rescue his long-lost uncle
from danger.

Also in Young Puffin

THE LITTLE WITCH

Margaret Mahy

Some stories are true, and some aren't...

Six surprising tales about sailors and pirates, witches and witch-babies, orphans and children, and even lions and dragons!

CANDY FLOSS AND IMPUNITY JANE

Rumer Godden

Candy Floss and Impunity Jane are two little dolls destined for adventure.

Pretty little Candy Floss belongs to Jack, the coconut-shy man. But horrible Clementina has her heart set on the doll and Candy Floss is in for some very unwelcome adventures!

Impunity Jane longs to have adventures and see the world, but the children who own her shut her up in a boring old dolls' house – until Gideon comes along.